Dos Niños
Two Children

Dedication

Este libro es dedicado a los donantes de órganos, a los destinatarios y a los doctores de Mayo Clinic quienes les sirven.

This book is dedicated to organ donors and recipients and the transplant teams at the Mayo Clinic who serve them.

Susurros del Espiritu Santo

Susurros del Espiritu Santo es una serie de libros que les proveen a los niños con respuestas espirituales a grandes preguntas. El texto de cada libro esta en Inglés y una segunda lengua de alrededor del mundo, en armonía con la Universalidad del espiritu humano. Cada libro está ilustrado por una artista empapada en la cultura de la segunda lengua.

Dos Niños es el trece libro en este serie. Los primeros dos de estos libros han sido publicados en tres idiomas. *The Villagers: Lílana Ageiraü* ha sido traducido tambien a Garifuna, uno de los idiomas nativos de Belice.

Whispers of the Holy Spirit

Whispers of the Holy Spirit is a series of books that provide children with spiritual answers to big questions. The text of each book appears in English and a second language from around the world, in keeping with the universality of the human spirit. Each is illustrated by an artist steeped in the second language's culture.

Dos Niños is the third book in this series. The first two of these books have already been published in three languages. *The Villagers: Lílana Ageiraü* is also translated into Garifuna, one of Belize's indigenous languages.

Published by Producciones de la Hamaca

Michael Resman, Author; Soonjung Han Hwang, illustrator; Elizabeth Pomroy, editor; Hyewon Grundy, Korean translator; 2015. *In the Land Beyond Living:* 사랑나 글호.

Michael Resman, Author; Cyrus Ngatia Gathigo, illustrator; Fred Senelwa, Swahili translator; 2012. *The Villagers: Wanakijiki.*

Michael Resman, Author; Cyrus Ngatia Gathigo, illustrator; Eldred Roy Cayetano, Garifuna translator; 2012. *The Villagers: Lílana Ageiraü.*

Dos Niños
Two Children

Historia por Michael Resman
Ilustrado por Clyde Kirkpatrick
Editado por Jayna Resman
Texto de español editado por Fabian Contreras
Translado por Frank Cummings, Marcial Alamina III, y Alma Novelo

Story by Michael Resman
Illustrated by Clyde Kirkpatrick
Edited by Jayna Resman
Spanish Editing by Fabián Contreras
Translated by Frank Cummings, Marcial Alamina III, and Alma Novelo

Whispers of the Holy Spirit #3

Producciones de la Hamaca
Caye Caulker, BELIZE

Copyright © 2016 Mike Resman
Illustrations: Copyright © 2016 Clyde Kirkpatrick

Other than as permitted by law, no part of this publication may be reproduced, stored in a retrieval system or transmitted, in any form by any means, without the prior written consent of the publisher or a licence from the Belize Copyright Licensing Agency. To obtain a licence from the Belize Copyright Licensing Agency, visit www.belizecopyright.com or its registered office 35 Elizabeth Street, Benque Viejo del Carmen, Belize Central America.

Published by *Producciones de la Hamaca*, Caye Caulker, BELIZE <producciones-hamaca.com>

ISBN: 978-976-8142-84-9 (print edition)
ISBN: 978-976-8142-85-6 (e-book edition)

Whispers of the Holy Spirit
ISBN: 978-976-8142-792

This book was printed on-demand by Lightning Source, Inc (LSI). The on-demand printing system is environmentally friendly because books are printed as needed, instead of in large numbers that might end up in someone's basement or a dump site. In addition, LSI is committed to using materials obtained by sustainable forestry practices. LSI is certified by Sustainable Forestry Initiative (SFI® Certificate Number: PwC-SFICOC-345 SFI-00980). The Sustainable Forestry Initiative is an independent, internationally recognized non-profit organization responsible for the SFI certification standard, the world's largest single forest certification standard. The SFI program is based on the premise that responsible environmental behavior and sound business decisions can co-exist to the benefit of communities, customers and the environment, today and for future generations <sfiprogram.org>.

Producciones de la Hamaca is dedicated to:
- Celebration and documentation of Belize's rich, diverse cultural heritage,
- Protection and sustainable use of Belize's remarkable natural resources,
- Inspired, creative expression of Belize's spiritual depth.

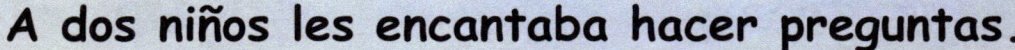

A dos niños les encantaba hacer preguntas.

Two children loved to ask questions.

Hacían preguntas simples "¿por qué tengo diez dedos en los pies?"

They asked little questions, "Why do I have ten toes?"

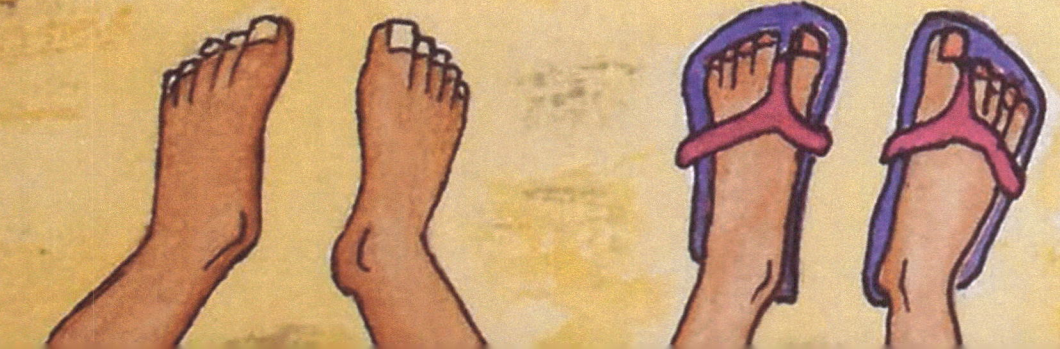

Y hacían preguntas grandes "¿a dónde se fue el ayer?"

And they asked big questions, "Where did yesterday go?"

Recibían respuestas a algunas de sus preguntas, a veces respuestas difíciles, a veces respuestas fáciles.

They got answers to some of their questions, sometimes hard answers and sometimes easy ones.

Encontraron una pregunta que era demasiado difícil "¿por qué estamos aquí?"

They found one question that was too big, "Why are we here?"

Mucha gente decía "nadie sabe la respuesta a eso."

Many people said, "No one knows the answer to that."

Entonces los niños dejaron de hacer esa pregunta, pero no dejaron de hacer muchas más.

So the children stopped asking that question and went on asking lots of others.

Con cada pregunta contestada, su conocimiento crecía y crecía.

With each question answered, their knowledge grew and grew.

Un día encontraron a una persona que no tenía prisa. Ella no solo les miró, sino también les miró dentro de cada uno de ellos.

One day they found a person who was not in a hurry. She didn't just look at them, but looked into each one of them.

Pudieron ver que ella era diferente, más profunda. Por eso decidieron hacerle la gran pregunta "¿por qué estamos aquí?"

The children could see that she was different, deeper. So they decided to ask her the big question, "Why are we here?"

Ella les sorprendió diciendo "me alegra que preguntaran eso. Les daré mi respuesta, pero necesitarán encontrar las suyas."

She surprised them by saying, "I'm glad you asked that. I will give you my answer, but you will need to find your own."

"Pueden ver mucho con sus ojos y entender mucho con sus mentes. Ahora usen el resto de ustedes para conocer. Agáchense y levanten algo. Si está vivo levántenlo cuidadosamente y procuren no hacerle daño."

"You can see much with your eyes and know much with your minds. Now let's use the rest of you to know. Bend down and pick something up. If it's alive, then pick it up gently and take care not to hurt it."

"Conózcanlo con sus corazones. Ámenlo. Ámenlo tan profundamente como sea posible."

"See it with your hearts. Love it. Love it as deeply as you can."

"Conózcanlo con sus almas. Ábranse. Ábranse al amor y sean uno con lo que está en sus manos. Sean uno con todas las cosas."

"See it with your souls. Open yourself. Open yourself to love and become one with what you're holding. Become one with all things."

Ella dijo "ahora que han visto con sus almas, aquí está mi respuesta. Miren a ver si también es la suya."

She said, "Now that you have seen with your souls, here is my answer. Look to see if it is also yours."

"Estamos aquí para ser misericordiosos, para hacer todo lo que podamos para ayudar a los demás."

"We are here to be merciful, to do all that we can to help others."

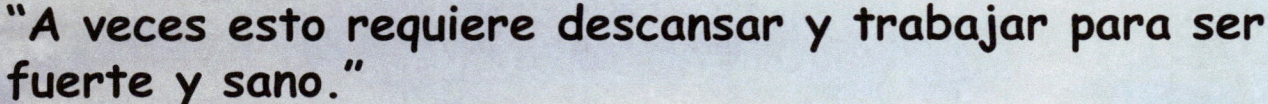

"A veces esto requiere descansar y trabajar para ser fuerte y sano."

"Sometimes this means resting and working to become strong and healthy."

"Por sobre todo, debemos servir a Dios."

"Above all, we must serve God."

"Hay un nombre para aquellos que dan misericordia. Es un nombre viejo, conocido por muchos: Ángeles."

"There is a name for those who bring mercy. It is an old name, known to many—Angels."

"Mírenme. Usen sus ojos espirituales y mírenme con sus almas." Ella se dio vuelta. "¿Pueden ver mis alas?" Con asombro, los niños asintieron "si."

"Look at me. Use your spiritual eyes, and see me with your souls." She turned around. "Can you see my wings?" In awe, the children nodded "yes."

"Ahora, mírense el uno al otro."

"Now, look at one another."

Asombrados, ellos se dieron cuenta de que ambos tenían alas espirituales y se llenaron de alegría.

Amazed, the children saw that they both had spiritual wings, and they were filled with joy.

"Fíjense," ella les dijo, "todos somos ángeles. Algunos escogen ayudar a los demás y compartir. Sus alas crecen grandes y fuertes."

"You see," she told them, "we are all angels. Some people choose to help others and share. Their wings grow large and strong."

"Algunos no usan sus alas, sino se atienden a ellos mismos."

"Some people don't use their wings, but instead serve only themselves."

"Ésta es la respuesta a su gran pregunta. Tiene la libertad de vivir como quiera."

"This is the answer to your big question. You are free to live as you wish."

Michael Resman

Durante mi vida profesional estuve al servicio de niños con capacidades diferentes como Terapista Ocupacional en una escuela pública. Ahora que estoy retirado, además de mis responsabilidades en la Iglesia Cuáquera, la oración y escribir se han convertido en mi vocación. Vivo con mi esposa y dos gatos en Rochester, Minnesota, EEUUA.

I spent my professional career serving children with disabilities as an Occupational Therapist in a public school. Now retired, in addition to other responsibilities in the Quaker church, prayer and writing have become vocations. I live with my wife and two cats in Rochester, Minnesota, USA.

Clyde Kirkpatrick

El artista ganador de premios Clyde Kirkpatrick ha pintado con acuarelas por más de 35 años. Su trabajo se ha mostrado en numerosas exposiciones y galerías, así como en colecciones privadas y de empresas en los Estados Unidos de Norteamérica y en el mundo. Ha enseñado arte y acuarelas en Universidades del Suroeste de Oregon. El y su esposa, Sharon, pasan ocho meses cada año en Belice donde enseñan de manera voluntaria pintura con acuarelas en las escuelas primarias de Cayo Hicaco y Cayo Ambergris.

Award-winning artist Clyde Kirkpatrick has been painting watercolours for more than 35 years. His work has been displayed in numerous shows and galleries, as well as in private and corporate collections in the United States and internationally. He has taught art and watercolour classes in colleges in southwest Oregon. He and his wife, Sharon, spend eight months of each year in Belize where he volunteers teaching watercolour classes in the primary schools of Caye Caulker and Ambergris Caye.

Susurros del Espiritu Santo

Susurros del Espiritu Santo es una serie de libros que les proveen a los niños con respuestas espirituales a grandes preguntas. El texto de cada libro esta en Inglés y una segunda lengua de alrededor del mundo, en armonía con la Universalidad del espiritu humano. Cada libro está ilustrado por una artista empapada en la cultura de la segunda lengua.

#1 *In the Land Beyond Living:* 사이라니 릏하 (Korean, publicado 2015) cuenta sobre que pasa antes de que nacemos.

#2 *The Villagers: Wanijiki* (Swahili, publicado 2012) ofrece una forma para llevarse bien con los demás.

#3 *Two Children: Dos Niños* (Spanish, publicado 2016) cuenta del porqué estamos a quien este tierra.

#4 *Oh God, Where Are You?* (Gaelic, programado 2017) habla del consuelo que Dios nos provee en tiempos dificiles.

#5 *Heaven* (Russian, programado 2018) nos a segura el perdón de Dios.

Whispers of the Holy Spirit

Whispers of the Holy Spirit is a series of books that provide children with spiritual answers to big questions. The text of each book appears in English and a second language from around the world, in keeping with the universality of the human spirit. Each is illustrated by an artist steeped in the second language's culture.

#1 *In the Land Beyond Living:* 사이라니 릏하 (Korean, published 2015) talks of what happens before we are born.

#2 *The Villagers: Wanijiki* (Swahili, published 2012) gives a way to get along with others.

#3 *Two Children: Dos Niños* (Spanish, published 2016) tells why we are here on this earth.

#4 *Oh God, Where Are You?* (Gaelic, scheduled 2017) speaks to God's comfort even in terrible times.

#5 *Heaven* (Russian, scheduled 2018) provides reassurance of God's forgiveness.

www.ingramcontent.com/pod-product-compliance
Lightning Source LLC
Chambersburg PA
CBHW042015150426
43196CB00002B/48